— CAPTIVE —
GEMS

AN ILLUSTRATED STORY
BY DAN KUBISHTA

1st edition, **Aug.** 2021

ISBN: **978-1-7376840-1-5**

Cover design by Dan Kubishta

THE SETTING

An island located on the Pacific Ocean is where this story is mostly set. It has many different residents, a large city, and vast nature reserves. The place is called Brisby and Canby, among other names, and often it is referred to as simply The Island. The people work hard there, making the place almost entirely self-sufficient. Cargo ships and cruise liners are seen regularly, and many events are held there. The climate is semi-tropical.

Chapter One
A Sunday in September

Penny Recovered

Penny had recovered. A small dog ran up to her in the backyard. Max smiled.

"Truly," said Suzanne. "These are the good days."

Paige came out of the house holding a tray of drinks. She brought them over to Max and Penny's mother, who promptly received them.

"Thank you, Paige," she said.

"Of course," said the well-groomed Price daughter.

2.

THE FIRST PHONE CALL

Paige's cell phone rang. She looked down at the screen. Unknown Number. She pressed ignore. The phone rang again.

"Excuse me," she said.

Leaving the backyard, Paige went into the house to take the call.

"Hello?"

"Paige?" came the exasperated reply.

"Yes, speaking," Evelyn-Paige replied evenly.

"It's Gerard," the voice said.

"Gerard," Paige reiterated.

Of course. How could she forget the romantic singer befriended by her sister, Colette?

"What's the matter," Paige said with her inherent class. "You sound nervous."

"Paige," Gerard said, "They've taken Colette."

3.

PAIGE AND SUZANNE

"I have to go," Paige told Max. Penny looked over. The dog nipped at her heels.

"What's the matter?" asked Suzanne. Max looked at his mother. Her age was showing when she spoke, the words full of melancholy.

"Long story," said Paige, handing a glass to Suzanne. The glass shone.

"I'll go with you," said Max.

"No," said Paige. "You have your life back here."

"Don't leave," said Penny.

"You've been very kind," Paige said to Suzanne.

"It's been nothing short of a dream," replied Suzanne.

4.

THE SECOND PHONE CALL

Paige closed her travel bag with a heavy thud. She took it and set it on the corner of the bed. The sun was setting outside, and a warm glow filled the guestroom.

Max stood at the door.

"What's the reason?"

"It's Colette," said Paige. "She's gone missing."

Max stood very still.

"Thank you for everything," Paige said. She was looking out the window with her back turned to Max. "I told you I couldn't stay long anyway. I still have plans to attend Ivy College in the fall."

"Yet you're going to Canby before?"

"I have to go," said Paige.

"What happens if you don't?"

"What happens if I don't?" Paige turned around and walked towards the bed. She placed her hand on the frame. Her phone sat on the bedside table.

"I don't know, but I want to be there if something does happen."

"How will you get there?"

Right then, the phone rang, and Max was startled. Paige took the phone and pressed answer.

"It's me again," Gerard said.

"I'm packing my bags, and I'll be there as quickly as I can."

"By cruise liner?"

"That's the way the Prices travel, and I don't want to end that now," Paige said with a bit of levity.

Max walked over to the window. The sunset was shining.

"Paige, I have a lead."

"I'm listening," she replied.

Max locked the window on the inside. The sound of the dog barking outside was muffled. Penny looked up to the window just in time to see Max turn away.

"I've intercepted some information with the help of Officer Lt. Tin," said Gerard.

"Yes, I know Tin," said Paige. "Old friend of my dad's."

Suzanne sipped lemonade in her glass as a Rolls-Royce appeared in the driveway.

"Tin says," Gerard continued, "That there was an altercation last night, the night Colette went missing."

Max leaned in to listen. Paige looked over at him. The white ribbon in her hair cascaded down her back.

"It was witnessed by one of his detectives."

"Where were you in all this?" Paige asked bluntly.

"Having a drink," Gerard responded with the most honest tone possible.

"Go on," Paige was now annoyed.

"Ms. Price! Ms. Price!"

The driver of the Rolls-Royce called with great gusto. Suzanne ran to the front to greet him. Paige left the room, briskly making her way down the spiral staircase of the house.

"The detective said that Colette was taken by a band of thieves."

5.

THE DETECTIVE

"A band of thieves," said the detective.

"Jams of a jillion options," said Officer Lt. Tin. Aldous looked over. They were all meeting at the law enforcement building on the island of Canby, about sixty miles off the coast of where Paige and Max now stayed.

"They demanded a ransom, Officer."

"Tell me more," said Lt. Tin, uncharacteristically intrigued.

6.
THE DISCLOSURE

Max followed Paige down the stairs. The Rolls-Royce was waiting.

"They asked for something that the detective could not provide," Gerard was saying.

"Just tell me!"

The driver put on sunglasses. Penny ran around to see what all the commotion was about.

"They wanted something that I have not heard a whisper about since I was a child."

Gerard had grown up on the island of Canby and was familiar with some of its lore.

"Gerard, just tell me." Paige was in the Rolls-Royce now, and Max stood outside of it. Suzanne joined him, and Penny was at her side. The dog growled.

"The Mermaid's Gem," said Gerard.

"The Mermaid's Gem?"

"Aye."

Max opened the door on the other side of the Rolls-Royce and hopped in.

"Max!"

"Max!"

"It's incredibly valuable," said Gerard, "and the last it was seen, it was in the possession of your family."

"I know," Paige affirmed. "It was my father's wedding gift to my mother."

7.

TO THE ISLAND

The driver was eager to leave. Suzanne took Penny's hand, and Max spoke to her out of the window.

"It was a good visit," said Max.

"I'll look forward to the next one," Suzanne said.

"You're not coming," said Paige.

"I am," said Max with a touch of bravado.

"The law enforcement building is where I'll be," Gerard said.

Paige nodded. She hung up the phone.

"Ready?" asked the driver.

Paige looked at Max.

"Fine," she said.

"Fine?" asked the driver.

"Ready," she replied quickly.

Penny waved. The car drove off.

8.

THE BAND

"Gerard," said Aldous professionally. "Colette raved about you. She positively loves you, and I had never seen her so happy in my entire life."

He sat across the young man at a pub. Officer Lt. Tin sat at the table too, keeping watch. Outside, pesky ravens flew about.

"You beat me to the punch with calling Paige," Aldous said, thanking the server who had just brought him a large soda.

"Normally, I would've made the call in a situation such as this, but nonetheless I thank you."

"You're very welcome, sir," Gerard responded genially. "She'll be here as soon as is possible. In the meantime..."

Officer Lt. Tin caught Gerard looking at him with a serious expression.

"I am law enforcement," Officer Lt. Tin responded, "But I am not a magic genie. I have no answers but the ones I seek out, and the answers I get are sometimes correct and sometimes wrong....but listen! I have had run-ins with the rapscallions what make mischief on this island countless times, and from your description? Gerard, it sounds as though this band is the gang known as the Uptown Pirates."

"Well, whatever they're known as, I don't care. They've taken Colette, and that's all that I am worried about. I've never met a finer woman."

"What would you do," Aldous said ominously, "For my daughter?"

"Whatever it takes, I will rescue her."

"I thought that you only just met her," Lieutenant Tin questioned.

"Yes," said Gerard. "It hasn't been long, it is true. I feel as though I've known her before the beginnings of the earth."

"Loverboy! Loverboy!"

It was an electronic parrot. Tin chuckled.

9.

THE ARRIVAL OF PAIGE AND MAX

"Hurry up," said Paige. Her pearl earrings bounced as she strode off her father's ship.

"I'm running as fast as I can."

Max took the luggage and had instant deja vu.

10.
Colette Captured

"I demand you to take me to the consulate."

Colette was in a cave. Across from her was a band of dirty, dirty thieves.

"I demand it!"

A young woman by the name of Libby was tied next to Colette. A person by the name of Ned Knight stood proudly in the middle of the cave.

"Finally," he said. "I've been freed of my captors. Arson was such a minor charge that I cannot believe I was actually imprisoned for it."

"First of all," said Colette. "You were not imprisoned. Second of all, you were not charged primarily for arson. You were charged primarily for striking Paige."

"Hitting a girl," said one of the thieves, "and you get sent to the workhouse."

"Quiet!" yelled Ned. "It's over now. I've learned my lesson. Do not cross Aldous."

He stooped to Colette's eye line.

"I'll save you," he whispered.

Colette didn't know what to say.

"This mermaid gem," said Libby. "You think I know where it is."

Colette struggled to get free.

"I know that it is somewhere within the Price's safekeeping," said one of the thieves. His name was Lion, and he had once worked for Aldous Price.

"The mermaid gem," he began.

The Mermaid Gem
It is a gem
That I have truly beheld
I saw it an eon ago, but still!
It was beautiful
When I saw it on the hand of Ms. Price
She held it a sconce
As I worked for the Fleet Owner
And I could not begin to bear it
When at my post
My poor, poor, poor, post
I had nothing, not even a parrot

So the gem!
It is my right,
A right I shall claim
For karma comes around once a decade
As for me, please listen up!
I will fill my king's cup

Captive Gems

Once the Mermaid's Gem is in my Possession

"Quiet!" said Ned. "I've told you to be quiet on numerous occasions."

"Ned, we were once comrades."

Ned remembered back to when Lion had looked on at a Bocce game he had bowled once in a park. Back then, Lion had been one of his cronies. Now though, Lion was the complete and absolute ruler of the thieves of Canby.

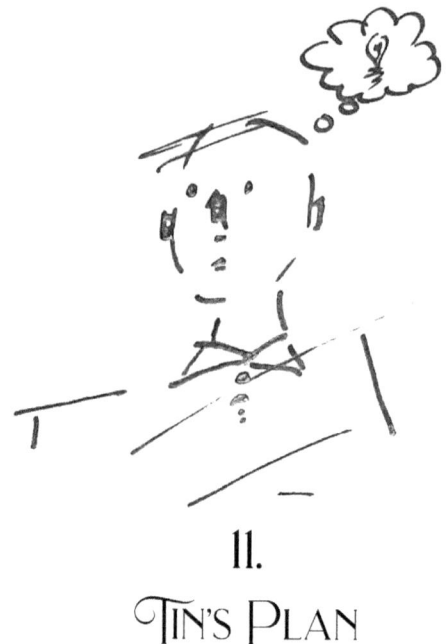

11.

TIN'S PLAN

"I daresay," Tin said as he swirled his newly grown mustache.

"This calls for more reconnaissance."

"More reconnaissance?"

"More reconnaissance!"

Gerard and Aldous followed Tin's lead. He motioned for them to leave the dining establishment, and soon they were boarding a car taking them back to the police station. A day passed. Another day passed. Ravens circled overhead. Gerard woke up and heard a knock on the door of the jailhouse. He had slept there, and he yawned.

Aldous entered the room.

"Where is the officer?" he asked.

"I think upstairs," came the reply.

Aldous sprinted up the steps.

Upon entering the upper level of the law enforcement building, Mr. Price saw Tin conversing with his detective friend.

"Timothy Green?" Aldous asked.

"At your service."

Mr. Green, known publicly as the owner of the island city's gem store, was also intelligence, so to speak.

12.
COLETTE'S SPEECH

Colette stood up. Ned was tied beside her, as was Libby still. The thieves were eating ridiculous amounts of chicken and mulled wine.

Outside of the cave, life went on as normal. The island's modern city was bustling with activity. The ports were active with cruise liners, and it seemed reminiscent of the city of Venice, except that the island was more tropical.

Colette shuffled her ankles, but still they were tied...no surprise. She tried to find the courage to speak, to say something, but all she could find was gasping noises. Lion turned around.

"I don't mean to be rude," he said, "but I know what I'm doing. There's no way that Aldous would have parted with that gem."

Colette stared at him. Libby did as well. Then, Colette began.

"Lion, is it?"

The thief looked at her. He had been smiling, but then his smile dropped.

"Lion, Lion. You've made one fatal flaw in your calculations. One that may cost you your life if you're not careful."

"If you have something to say, missy, say it."

The rest of the thieves gathered around, mysteriously drawn to Colette's words. They were disheveled.

"On the night when I was abducted, there was someone with me, if you recall. Someone that you did not expect. His name is Gerard, and he is my boyfriend. Now, Gerard is an extremely astute individual. He may not look it, but I assure you, he's one smart cookie. Now!

29

Listen. You will listen. There is not a person on this island who does not know my name, and there is no chance that I will not be rescued. You know this, or I shall call you a liar. Furthermore…"

13.

A GOOD CONSPIRACY

"Okay," said Paige. She, Max, Tin, Aldous, Gerard, and Timothy Green sat in a circle. Mr. Green stood up.

"The mermaid gem? The mermaid gem? This is ridiculous."

Mr. Price straightened his tie.

"The thieves do not want the mermaid gem. They want power, in any way they can get it. The mermaid gem is a cipher."

"Explain," said Tin, mildly annoyed.

"You see," said Mr. Green, his presence casting a shadow on everyone in the party except maybe the officer, "There is no special significance to the mermaid gem. I ought to know, for I was the one who sold it to Aldous here so long ago."

"Are you saying you sold me a faulty jewel? That was meant to be for my woman, you know. I feel slighted," said Aldous sadly.

"No!" cried Timothy, "That's not exactly what happened, my friend. The jewel, this mermaid gem, was indeed valuable at the time."

"What's your point?" Max cut in. Everyone in the room looked at him.

"I mean to say," Max flushed red, "That I offer my services, but I don't understand anything you're all talking about."

"I shall explain," said Tin.

He stood up, stretched, and polished the button on his suit with a piece of cloth.

"Many years ago, I was just a young lieutenant in training. Aldy here was with me. While I went on to become the man you see today, Aldy went on to become the fleet owner that *he* is today. It is no miracle that we have retained our friendship, for it was forged early on."

Aldous rolled his eyes.

"Do not monologue," he said.

"Right," said Tin with his characteristic accent. "There was the lovely Kendra, whom some of you knew."

Paige smiled.

"Kendra and Aldy were set to be married on the most fabulous ship I have ever seen. I recommended that Aldy get his lady a beautiful gem from Mr. Green, and so he did. So he did."

"The mermaid gem," said Max.

"Yes!"

The whole group laughed, but then realized they were dealing with serious business.

"Every second we squabble is another second Colette is in peril," Gerard reminded them.

"We shall find her soon enough. There is a reason that we have been slow to act." It was Mr. Green.

"What?" asked Paige.

"I said, there is a reason we have been slow to act."

A creak was heard. Above them was a pair of eyes looking down through the rafters, peering out from the gloom.

"We're being watched," said Mr. Price quietly.

"Lion, is that you?" Gerard asked.

"No," came the narrow reply. "It is his ambassador."

"Show yourself, coward," said Tin.

While the spy surrendered, dropping down through the rafters like a spider, the story continued.

"Aldy loved Kendra, and so he kept the gem long after her departure. In fact, he has it with him, do you not?"

"Yes," said Aldous. "It's in my briefcase, along with all of my important papers."

"Listen," came the shrill voice that was coming from the spy. "I bring a message from Lion."

"We're listening," the whole group said together.

"The message that I got from Lion is that we's be needing that gem, now."

Tin grabbed a pair of handcuffs and locked the fool up.

14.

BACK TO COLETTE

"Listen," Lion said. "I hear the song of the sirens."

It was true. Colette, Libby, and Ned looked over.

THE SEA LASS SINGS
A SEPULCHRAL SONG
THAT WEAVES AROUND THE EARTH
"DO NOT CRY," GO THE WORDS

"FOR IF YOU DO, THERE WILL BE A GIANT PROBLEM."

Then Colette sang.

BRISTOL'S BLUE EYES
HAD BEEN FULL OF SURPRISE
SINCE THAT MORNING IN TRUE BLUE SEPTEMBER
THEN SHE HAD BEEN TROUBLED
AS THE GUEST LIST HAD DOUBLED
TO MORE THAN COULD BE REMEMBERED

There were only three thieves in addition to Lion that still made camp in the cave.

"You see," said Lion. "I am not a violent person. That is why you have not been killed. I always get what I want, though. Soon, I will be the king of the island."

Ned rolled his eyes. At one time, he too had wanted to rule, but reality

37

smashed his dreams and led him to a new perspective.

"Tell me, Lion," said Colette, chewing on a biscuit, "How much longer will you wait?"

"Until your father shows his face."

"My father?"

15.

LION'S BACKSTORY

The reason for Lion's motivation was simple. He wished to exact revenge on the father of Colette and Paige, and in so doing would remedy his long-gestating emotions toward the fleet master. Back in the day, he had worked for Price Fleets, but had been promptly fired. Years later, he had brought to fruition his plan of kidnapping the daughter of Colette to bring the gem to himself.

"Why do you want the mermaid gem?"

Lion hid his face.

16.
THE TEAM

The spy had let the cat out of the bag. It was really quite easy. Tin was intimidating when he wanted to be, and it was not hard to extract information from the squabbling thief.

"They let their guard down at four in the morning," the officer said.

Max ate a doughnut. The team was now assembled outside of the law enforcement building. Paige, her father, Max, Gerard, Mr. Green, Lt. Tin, and the thief were all dressed in blue uniforms with shining buttons. Paige slapped the thief across the face.

"What have you done with my sister?" she demanded.

"It wasn't me, it wasn't me," the pathetic thief tried to explain. "It was the king, it was Lion. Lion. Lion."

"Lion it was," said Gerard. "I saw."

"Lion, Lion, Lion," Paige repeated. She tied her hair up into a bun with a white ribbon. "What a name."

"It's real," said Aldous. "I remember the rascal, and I remember firing him."

He gripped his briefcase. Inside was the mermaid gem.

"You will lead us to Colette," Tin said.

The spy groveled.

Tin stood up. He dialed a number.

"Hello?" It was Lion.

"Yes, hello Lion."

"Who is this?"

"My name is Grover," said Tin.

"Grover?"

Lion hung up the phone.

Above Tin, a raven screamed.

"My mistake," said Tin.

He redialed the phone. This time, he held it up to the spy.

"You will speak," said Aldous.

Lion didn't answer.

17.

REALIZATION

Lion put the cell phone in his pocket.

"That's my phone," said Libby.

"Quiet! Where's Ian."

Colette smiled.

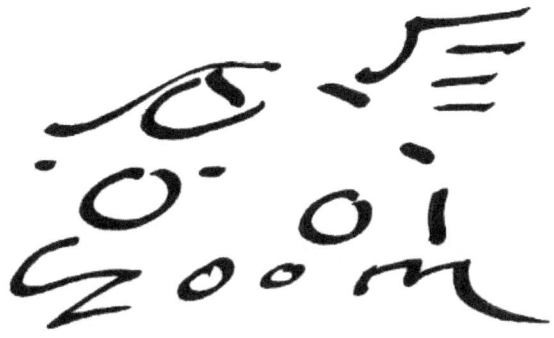

18.

TURNING POINT

Sirens blared. Kat, Max's aunt, looked out of a window. She had been working diligently at her inn, The Dazing Inn, and had just received a call from her sister, Suzanne.

"Keep a lookout for Max," said Suzanne.

"He's back on the island?" asked Kat.

"Yes, last I checked."

"Oh!"

Liliane Camden, the secretary of Kat's, typed something on a typewriter from the 40s. Literally outside, Tin's Aston Martin sped down the street. He drove. Aldous and the rest of the gang sat in the car, silently awaiting confrontation.

"The mermaid gem, the mermaid gem," sang Lion.

"Why did you kidnap me?" Libby asked.

"I didn't kidnap you. You were with Colette. I am frustrated that you do not remember."

"Tell me," she said.

"Why must I? Let me finish this song, and then I will tell you, if I'm in the mood."

Lion began to croon. The chains of Colette's binding were exact.

The Mermaid Gem
The Mermaid Gem
I say that I desire it
No, it's not true,
I do not care

Captive Gems

For I am not a pirate
The Mermaid Gem
The Mermaid Gem
There is no reason for me
To love it! Only fools love rocks
No, I am in it for the sport of it

The Aston Martin flew through the city.

"I am tired," said Lion.

Ned had his hands bound.

"I never should've associated with you jokers," he said.

"Well, you did. Say, where's that old crown you used to wear around?"

Just then, the cave was invaded.

"This is a complete rescue," screamed Tin, his mustache bristling with hilarious power. The team was assembled. They shone like gemstones.

"Finally!" said Lion. He looked at Aldous. "I knew you'd come."

Aldous threw the mermaid's gem at Lion, who caught it midair. All of the

47

thieves ran away, save Ian the spy. Paige punched Lion in the face. He toppled over, the mermaid gem falling into a crack on the cave's stone floor. Aldous thought of his wife as he beheld the beloved gem falling to the center of the earth. He wept.

"Aldous! Aldous!" roared Lion.

Paige untied Colette and Libby. When she got to the third person, she was surprised.

"Ned?"

"I have been a jerk for as long as I can remember," he said. "Now, I know who's side I'm on. I will never betray the Prices again, not while I still have a sliver of conscience."

"People do change," said Timothy Green.

19.

THE TRUTH

Lion stood face to face with Mr. Price. Colette, Ned, Libby, Paige, Timothy, Gerard, Ian, Tin, and Max stood in a line near them. Water from the ocean came into the cave periodically. A crab washed up and bit Lion on the ankle.

"No!" he said.

LET'S BEGIN OUR QUARREL
TEN YEARS IN THE WORKS

You were once my master
With all the perks
Although now I stare at you
With dread,
I must say
I'm glad you're here
For you, Mr. Price
Have no fear

Paige stepped forward.

"Step down, daughter!" Mr. Price ordered.

"Absolutely not. I stand with you."

"As do I," said Colette.

Lion snarled.

"I never wanted the gem. It was never about the gem."

Tin looked at the cave floor. Aldous had set his briefcase on its bosom earlier when he had gone to confront Lion.

All of a sudden, a gust of wind swept through the cave. Lion ran to the briefcase, seizing it. Paige ripped the ribbon out of her hair. Tin fired two blanks.

50

"Tell me," Aldous cried, lifting his hands above his head, "Did you think you could so easily cross the most powerful man on Canby?"

Ned gulped. "Never cross Aldous," he said.

Aldous cracked his knuckles. Lion shined his shoes.

"Here it goes," said Tin.

"Give me the briefcase back," Aldous said. He pulled out a weapon.

"Give me my station back," Lion retorted.

"My briefcase."

"My station."

"My briefcase."

"My station."

Paige slipped away. Colette followed. Libby crept up behind Lion, Tin and Max stood at the side of Aldous, and Timothy Green went back out to the Aston Martin. Gerard threw platitudes at Colette. Ian tied his shoes.

"My briefcase."

"My station."

Ned crawled on all fours towards Lion. Aldous held his breath.

Bristol's orange eyes had been full of surprise a voice sang.

Lion looked around.

One
Two
Three
Four
Five
Six
Seven

"My briefcase."
"My station."

Eight
Nine
Ten

Just like that, Aldous razed Lion to the ground, recovered the briefcase, and rushed out to the Aston Martin. Libby

52

tied Lion's hands, Tin and Max escorted him out of the cave, and all was won.

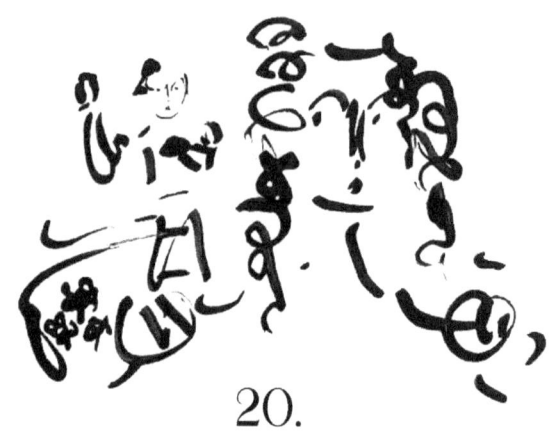

20.

LIBBY AND KAT

"Thank you so much for your hospitality," said Libby.

"Anytime, young lady," said Kat.

Libby's green eyes shone. She walked out of the Dazing Inn's parlor and onto the front lawn. Max, Paige, Colette, and Gerard sat around a white table eating mixed bowls of fruit. Libby went to join them, and soon after left to meet a friend.

"Say hello to Rose for me!" said Max.

"Will do," Libby said.

21.

THE FEAST

Music blasted. Tin, Timothy, and Aldous threw a feast at the park rivaling the island's annual gala.

"Peace is restored," said Tin.

They laughed.

22.
THE END

Max sat on a rocky bluff overlooking the ocean. Paige sat nearby, and so did Colette and Gerard.

"It's getting late," said Max.

The sun had set, and a slight breeze whispered across the shore.

"Shall we?"

The four trotted up a hill.

"Evelyn-Paige," said Colette. "Never a dull moment."

Gerard was silent.

Above them, in the sky, the stars were beginning to appear. They shone.

Captive Gems

Dan Kubishta lives and works on the West Coast, U.S.A. *Captive Gems* is his fourth book.